The Mindfulness Room

Written by Amanda Lynch

Edited by Candice L. Davis

Be Mindful

ISBN: 978-0-578-53381-0
LCCN: 2019909757

This book is dedicated to my grandparents, Mrs. Beulah Davis, Rev. John E. Gordon, Sr. & Mrs. Violet P. Gordon. Thank you for filling me with resiliency, strength, and courage. I am who I am because of you.

To my parents Carl B. Davis, Sr., Sandra Peterson, Carolyn Edghill, and Bernard Peterson, thank you for your unconditional love and your belief that I was anointed and called to do great things. Thank you for encouraging me to stay true to myself and to live a purpose-driven life. You all never gave up your belief that I could do anything that I imagined. Thank you for always seeing greatness inside of me. There was nothing that you wouldn't have given me, even if it came at great sacrifice to you. I love you to the moon and back and I hope I've made you proud.

Special thank you also goes to my sister and editor, Candice L. Davis, whose words of wisdom helped to carry me through this journey. To my best friend, Angel J. Jackson, whose beautiful life was tragically cut short, your friendship is never far away from my heart and your spirit lives through My'Angel. Finally, to my husband, Marcus, and my children, Justin, Ava, Hazy, and Rosebud, thanks for always encouraging me to be better.

My name is My'Angel Trent. I live in the Ivy Court housing community.

Last year, my daddy passed away. That made my mama so sad. Sometimes she has a hard time getting out of bed. I haven't seen her smile or laugh since that day. She loved my daddy so much. We all did.

Now my mama looks sad a lot and doesn't spend as much time with us. She lost her job after that. I would do anything to see Mama smile again.

I tell her jokes, tickle her toes, and even do pranks around the house, but she's still so sad all the time. She used to be so much fun.

I don't know what else to do. I guess I don't smile much anymore myself. I'm just glad summer break is over and we're going back to school. In our neighborhood, it's not safe to play outside, but I can play at school.

I can't wait to see my old teacher, Ms. Criswell! She's short like me and smells like flowers. We have so much fun in her class! Her room is decorated like some place called Paris. She's always dreamed of going there. She says we should have big dreams too!

On the first day of school, I run to Ms. Criswell's class, but she isn't there. She had a baby and moved to some place called Pennsylvania.

My new teacher, Ms. Williams, says, "Ms. Criswell told me all about you!" Ms. Criswell told her I'm really smart and I like to dance. Ms. Criswell also told her I get sad sometimes. Ms. Williams says, "We can work on that together."

Every morning, she meets me outside our classroom door and does a special dance with me. She does special things with all the kids in our class. Some get special handshakes. Some get hugs. I always get to dance.

Ms. Williams introduces me to a new lady at our school. Her name is Mrs.Lynch, and she can help me with my sadness too. She teaches something called mindfulness and yoga.

"That sounds like fun," I tell her, but the truth is I don't even know what yoga is.

As I walk into Mrs. Lynch's class, that crazy lady is doing a headstand! She has bright red hair, and she's wearing jeans!

What kind of teacher wears jeans and does headstands in the classroom? She's also the first teacher I've ever seen who's brown like me.

Mrs. Lynch stands on her feet when we come in the door. "Hey, baby cakes! I'm Mrs. Lynch, and I heard you're a scholar, young queen!"

She asks if she can give me a big hug, and I say yes. She smells a lot like the cakes Mama used to make with me. She asks if I want to come and have lunch with her, and she says I can bring my sister, Leila, if I want.

Mrs. Lynch's room sounds like the ocean. She has a big glowing rock on her desk. She doesn't have any desks for kids in her room. Instead, she has small pillows on the floor and some rolled-up mats in the corner. What kind of classroom is this? It's the Mindfulness Room.

Ms. Lynch and I have so much fun at Lunch Bunch with Leila, and instead of sitting at tables, we sit "criss-cross applesauce" on a cushion.

She asks us questions about our family and about things we like to do. I tell her my daddy died and my mama is sad all the time. I tell her I'm sad a lot too. She asks if she can call Mama to talk about my sadness, and I say I'm fine with that.

After we finish eating lunch, Mrs. Lynch asks us to draw a picture of someplace where we feel safe. I draw a picture of me with my daddy at Chimborazo Park. I miss him so much.

Before we leave, Mrs. Lynch shows us a quick trick. She asks us to breathe in through our noses while we push our bellies out.

She tells us to hold the breath for five seconds and then blow like we're blowing out a birthday candle. She tells us to do that five times. She calls it breath work.

Mrs. Lynch says if we feel sad or anxious, we can try breath work until we felt safe again. She says this will help us listen to our bodies.

"Next time," Mrs. Lynch says, "We'll try doing it with our eyes closed, but only if you're comfortable."

I'm not too sure about that.

Next time, I try breath work with my eyes closed, and it's great. I love the Mindfulness Room!

Every day, I go to Mrs. Lynch's room to do breath work, and I start to feel happy again.

My favorite days are when we do Chicken Breathing. That always makes me laugh because we look so silly.

I show other kids in my class how to listen to their bodies and to breathe when they feel angry or sad.

Mrs. Lynch even helps my teacher laugh and breathe more. Sometimes we eat fruit, chocolate, and other yummy food very slowly with Mrs. Lynch.

Sometimes we walk outside like we have dinosaur feet.

Sometimes we color mandala sheets.

Sometimes we raise our eyebrows as high as we can to stretch our faces.

Mrs. Lynch says all these things are tools for our mindfulness kits. These are tools inside my brain to help me calm down when my body feels busy or sad. These tools help me make good choices and pay attention.

One day, a friend of Mrs. Lynch comes to school to play the drums with us. We have a junkyard jam to get rid of the junk that made us sad.

I even invite my mama to come and learn to breathe and laugh with me. She says, "Go 'head somewhere, girl!" One day, Mama changes her mind, and Leila and I teach her how to walk like a dinosaur.

The neighbors look at us like we're crazy because we walk to the bus stop like we have dinosaur feet. Mama looks so funny! I can't stop laughing at the look on her face while she stretches her neck like a dinosaur and walks like she has gigantic feet.

This is the first time I've seen my mama smile in a long time. It makes me so happy to see her happy, even just for a second. "I've missed your smile," I tell Mama.

She grabs me tightly and says, "I've missed your smile too, My'Angel."

I also teach my mama how to breathe like a chicken! That really makes us laugh. The next time she feels sad, she's going to stop and breathe like a chicken, even if she's at the grocery store.

Mrs. Lynch and a social work lady meet with Mama, and sure enough, Mama begins to laugh and smile more. We start doing breath work together every night before bed.

I still miss my daddy a lot, but I know he's happy to see Mama, Leila, and me smiling again.

Strategies from the Mindfulness Room

Dear Readers,

The practice of mindfulness helps us to build our working memory, reduce stress and anxiety, and lower blood pressure. Prior to using this work with children, it is essential that you establish your own personal practice. For me, that involves daily walks through nature. For others, like my husband, it might mean kickboxing. There are specific strategies you can employ that will help you to build mindfulness into your daily routine. Remember that everyone's "soul work" looks different. Here are some of the strategies mentioned in the book that you may find useful as you develop your own practice with your students or even with your own children.

I introduce mindfulness to my students by first talking about "big feelings," which may include sadness, anger, happiness, frustration, and fear. We frequently use a Feelings Wheel to help guide those conversations. Your job as the safe adult is to connect, build relationships, and invite your students to implore mindful practices, such as those listed on the following pages, when they are experiencing "big feelings."

Mindfulness Room ABC's

A-Awareness: Your breath is always present and always changing. This makes it an ideal focal point for meditation. It's best to have students spend five to ten minutes a day in meditation to develop the habit. Teach students to access controlled breathing and mindful practices before they need them during times of stress or crisis. Model those practices and talk about them during class meetings and with parents. Breath work helps students build social and emotional skills and learn how to listen to their bodies. Begin with two to three minutes of helping students find their diaphram. From there, invite students to inhale and exhale using belly breathing.

B-Belly Breathing (diaphragmatic breathing): Belly breathing is a calming skill you can use if you're feeling anxious or when you need to quiet your mind. Invite students to breathe deeply, inhaling by using their diaphragm to push their stomach out rather than using the muscles of their chest to fill the lungs.

C-Chicken Breath (dynamic breathing): Chicken breath looks ridiculous, and that's why it's perfect for students to learn. This should be taught in three parts. First, remind students to keep their mouths closed during this activity so they won't become dizzy. Have them stand up and begin by taking a deep breath very quickly and in rapid succession. Next, instruct them to bend their arms and pump them up and down (like a bellow) while they breathe. Their arms should look like wings, but they shouldn't be loose or flappy. They should be strong. Your arms go up as you inhale and down as you exhale. Lastly, guide the students to bend their knees as they exhale and bring their arms down, then straighten their legs as they inhale. This practice can be done for one to three minutes. Upon completion, invite students to return to center by closing their eyes and drawing their attention back inward. After they finish, have them continue to stand for a minute to reflect on how their bodies feel.

D-Dinosaur Feet: Walking meditation helps students who get anxious or can't sit still. In this case, the focus is on your feet, not your breath. Invite students to close their eyes and stand behind their chairs. Have them walk slowly left to right, rolling their ankles and wiggling their toes. Next, have them walk slowly in place, and then begin to walk slowly with their awareness fully engaged in the sensations in their feet. Students should walk slowly and in silence for three to five minutes. Students can also roll or extend their necks while engaged in this practice.

E-Eating: Begin by talking about the benefits of mindful eating. First, have students sit comfortably in the criss-cross-applesauce position and bring their awareness to the food object they've been given. I typically use grapes, oranges, dark chocolate, peppermints, and/or lemons.

Invite them to activate their five senses to notice the texture, color, or the smell of the object.

Guide them to chew the object very slowing, taking note of the taste, sensation, and texture of the food. At the conclusion of this activity, talk about what they've observed.

F-Focus: Invite students to close their eyes during meditation. Some may be apprehensive about closing their eyes for a variety of personal reasons. Allow them the choice to soften their gaze on a focal point.

G-Gratitude: Encourage your students to find the goodness in their day. You can have them write down things they're grateful for and drop them into a gratitude jar. During times of challenge, have them pull a slip from their gratitude jar to remind them of things they were thankful for during a more peaceful or grounded time.

H-Heart: Your heart is at the center of your body. The heart meditation allows you to rest your attention, while breathing slowly and focusing on your heartbeat. Have students spend three to five minutes focusing on their heartbeat while slowly breathing from their bellies. This helps with focus and with setting daily intention.

I-Inhale and Exhale (Pranayama): Breathing exercises are a great way to start and end each day. Helping students learn to control their breathing has many health benefits such as a reduction in stress and improved concentration. Some students may inhale from their chest instead of their bellies and these students often hold stress in their bodies. It takes practice to retrain your breath, and students may need reminders to breathe properly.

J-Judgment Free: Encourage students to release any judgments they have about meditation and mindfulness. This work takes practice, but it works! If they find their minds are wandering, have them label those thoughts and release them.

K-Kindness: Practice and model kindness toward yourself and others. Self-compassion is key when learning to meditate.

L-Lion Breath (Simhasana): Lion breath helps to reduce stress because it allows you to stretch your entire face. Lion breath can be done while seated in a chair, in criss cross applesauce style on the floor, or on a cushion or bolster. Students look up at the ceiling, open their mouths as wide as they can, and stick their tongues out as far as they will go, curling their tongues downwards. Next, they exhale forcefully while making a "haaaa" sound. Repeat for three to five minutes.

M-Mandala: A mandala is a repetitive design drawn inside a circle. There are many different forms of mandalas readily available via Internet search engines and at your local bookstore. Having students color in this pattern helps to reduce stress and promotes relaxation and mind balance.

N-Nature: Find time to have students connect with nature. Take walks outside and make observations about the things you see and hear while focusing on your breathing.

O-Ocean Breath (Ujjayi Pranayama): Invite your students to exhale by fogging up a mirror or glass. They should hear a hissing sound that sounds similar to ocean waves. Next, invite them to contract their throat muscles the same way on the inhale breath. When they are able to control their throat on both the inhale and exhale, invite them to practice ocean breath with their mouths closed on both the inhale and exhale. This breathing pattern helps to calm the body's fight or flight response and can be used to as a focus point for seated meditations.

P-Practice: Meditation takes practice. Find ten to fifteen minutes each day to build your own personal practice before introducing mindfulness to students.

Q-Quiet: Designate a distraction-free zone where you can focus on quiet and stillness when beginning your mindfulness practices. Eliminate environmental distractions when you can.

R-Relationships: Relationships matter. Simply put, kids don't work for teachers they don't like. Developing a mindfulness practice takes a lot of trust and openness between the student and the teacher. We're asking students to be vulnerable and to embark on something they haven't been exposed to in the past. In order for this to work, we have to invest in learning about our students and in developing trusting relationships with them.

S-Stillness Meditation: Find a quiet space to relax and quiet your mind. If you find your thoughts wandering, simply label and release them.

T-Time: This work takes time. Be kind to yourself. There's no right or wrong way to meditate. Keep in mind that developing resilience and mindfulness is a process and not an overnight change.

U-Understanding: Understand that students may be apprehensive about developing a mindfulness practice. They may be uncomfortable sitting in silence or even closing their eyes for a variety of reasons. Make adjustments where you need to. Not everyone's "soul work" will be the same.

V-Village: Create a supportive village around you that encourages you to commit to your daily practice. It takes a village to create change.

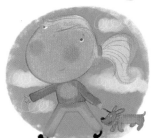

W-Walking Meditation: Walking meditation allows students to make mind-body connections through walking and making observations about their environment. It can be done at any speed (even while running) and is designed to bring your awareness to the space around you.

X-Exercise: Encourage students to exercise for at least thirty minutes a day. Studies show that even thirty minutes of low-impact exercise helps to improve physical, emotional, and mental health.

Y-Yoga: Yoga is a group of spiritual, physical, and emotional practices that improve your strength, flexibility, and focus. The breathing techniques and poses can help reduce toxic stress and anxiety in students.

Z-Zen Gardens: Zen gardens afford students the opportunity to quietly and calmly sweep sand using a miniature or tabletop sand garden. This helps students relax and focus. Zen gardens can be kept at workstations, centers, or even inside students desks.

Author Amanda Lynch, MA, CTP-E, is an Educational Consultant specializing in Self-Care, Mindfulness-Based Trauma-Informed Practices, and Restorative Justice.

She is a licensed teacher and has worked in public education for nearly twenty years. Currently, she provides professional development workshops throughout the United States for educators, students, and families on the impact of Adverse Childhood Experiences (ACES) on student and family engagement and on learner cognition.

She loves introducing communities of color to mindful practices, meditation, yoga, and sound healing therapy.

She lives with her husband, Marcus, and her very busy children, Justin, Ava, Hazy and Rosebud, in Glen Allen, Virginia.

She is also the founder of Rethinking Resiliency LLC.